King David Dances

Also by Francis Stuart from New Island Books:

Poetry: *We Have Kept the Faith: Poems 1918—1992*
Arrow of Anguish

Fiction: *The Pillar of Cloud*
Redemption

FRANCIS STUART

King David Dances

NEW
ISLAND
BOOKS

DUBLIN

King David Dances

is first published in 1996

in Ireland by

New Island Books,

2 Brookside,

Dundrum Road,

Dublin 14,

Ireland.

ISBN 1 874597 44 8

New Island Books receives financial assistance from

The Arts Council (An Chomhairle Ealaíon),

Dublin, Ireland.

Cover design by Jon Berkeley

Typeset by Graphic Resources

Printed in Ireland by Colour Books, Ltd.

For Madeleine in Memoriam

I would like to acknowledge here the great help I received from John de Paor in advising me on many of the Biblical details in this novella, besides lending me books on the subject.

F . S .

We were a few days in Jerusalem before going north to Megiddo, and there I confirmed what I had surmised: my guide and companion's status in the state of Israel was not an unimportant one. Joshua had a certain, if limited, support in the Knesset of which he was an elected member, but it was on the streets of the larger towns that he exerted power with his so-called Corps of Vigilantes. This was a gang of toughs but as they had fought gallantly in the Seven (or was it Five?) Days War they had not, as yet, been outlawed. Joshua, however, had spent a brief period in a disused wing of the Tel Aviv penitentiary. This I heard not from Joshua but from his girl Micaah whom he met there where she had run into him, as she put it, in a passage, and copulated, as she also put it, on the spot.

At Megiddo things went wrong. I didn't know why and then I realised it was Joshua. One of my most publicised achievements had been the exploration of the underground water systems of the cities of Judaea and Samaria. At Megiddo there were also the amazing above-ground constructions, such as the stables of Solomon which were neither stables nor had much to do with Solomon. The city had originally been supplied with water from a well outside the walls. Then a shaft had been sunk in the city itself and within it a spiral stone stairway wide enough to let donkeys laden with water jars and led by women pass each other and ending in a tunnel a hundred-and-forty feet underground that led to the well.

Joshua was unhappy at Megiddo: it was Ahab's city and this great king had seemed determined to diminish or ignore the Judaic traditions which Joshua revered.

Joshua's good humour returned however when we were in the semi-desert. He was obsessed by the wells, showing me several and giving them their biblical names, including Jacob's.

Then, on one of these excursions we stopped at a stone hut, if that's not a contradictory term, inhabited by an old couple, Nathan and Shebah, Arabs, Joshua told me. There we spent a few days at his suggestion, to which as I was in no particular hurry I agreed. Perhaps I felt that he had a purpose in this beyond taking me to more wells surrounded often by acacia groves and to an imposing Byzantine-Roman ruin.

One morning when he was still asleep in his jeep and Nathan was watering his flock, yes I slip instinctively into biblical language at this point, the woman, Shebah, after brewing a jug of coffee (a truck from I don't know where on its way to Haifa delivered provisions irregularly) took me by the hand, or rather wrist, as if I might try to break away, and led me down a shallow flight of stone steps from the sanded floor of the living room into a small cellar dimly lit by a burning wick in an oil jar.

On a low table, although looking back I see it as an altar, rested a box four-feet long by two-and-a-half-feet wide. When I looked up the measurements in the Pentateuch, a copy of which in Hebrew I had as usual with me, I found the measurements to be slightly less.

There were flakes of a dullish yellow metal on the wood that, without touching it, I took to be cedar. These were all that were left of the gold overlay. I sensed that had I touched it with a fingertip, it would have crumbled into a gritty dust.

I had been shown the unique Ark of the Covenant and all later doubts could not cause the vision to dissolve.

Oh, I had all sorts of explanations, more incredible than what my senses reported. Had Shebah put a portion of mandrake root into my coffee, the drug that Leah, or her son, had brought in from the field for Jacob?

Later I spent hours up in the attic looking up the passage in which "the Ark of the Covenant" or "the Ark of the Lord" is mentioned in Genesis, Kings, Deuteronomy and the Book of Samuel.

In the latter I read and then re-read this: 'David wearing a linen ephod danced without restraint before the Ark of the Lord' (2 Sam. 6:14-20). Michal, Saul's daughter, said to him: "'What a glorious day for Israel when he exposes his person in the sight of his servants' slave girls like any empty-headed fool.'"

Michal's father had been the first king of Israel before David had succeeded to the throne.

I meditated on how Jehovah's token of his promise to the once chosen people had stood in the Holy of Holies in the temple at Jerusalem flanked by candelabra under the spread wings of cherubim in the form described by Ezekiel.

That's when I became unbalanced, lost touch with what passes for reality. If I made public my discovery, would my name find its place among those of the mystics? Or the philosophers, or physicists? Heidegger, Einstein, Wittgenstein?

Of course I couldn't hide my state of mind. My behaviour was eccentric by suburban and even urban standards. There was Sabra's funeral, a small one of half-a-dozen cars in which my few faithful friends attended. Sabra, who was my sole companion for a number of years, was a pale coloured cat, and when the funeral had driven slowly round the suburban block, she was buried, after I had recited a short prayer, in the garden.

There were, naturally, other events, judged by some of the neighbours from eccentric (Dominique: *vous êtes bizarre, vous!*) to "round the bend" and plain crazy.

Some of my relatives, again not all, testified with examples from the past. It was said I took a carpet sweeper to the front lawn because I had a lawn mower that hovered an inch or so above the grass.

What, among a multiplicity of other things, it comes to is that the consensus, the generally held assumptions, of this age and place, are so erroneous that to share them even semi-consciously constitutes a personal disaster.

How did I manage to escape it? Partly and luckily by temperament and partly by spending much of my time in the Middle East which, besides being more heterogeneous and less consensus-prone, is, along with having serious disadvantages, also in touch with tradition and one of the great periods of the past.

All wasn't well, with me — "and never has been", yes, reader, you've got it right. And yet what blessings, long-, medium- and short-term: a prophet to whom a unique revelation had been given, a famed archaeologist and Old Testament scholar, about to make love to a wonderful woman, no mean hand as a chef, especially in the way of fish, and, withal, I have omitted what in the eyes of God are probably my best chances of what was once called "salvation". Such as my care and protection of Sabra and Sabrina.

Doesn't that bring us back to Heidegger with his postulate that the vital vision, the true astonishment we can assimilate with our morning coffee? Of course he puts it in his own superb way, have I noted, have *you*, that he was one of the great interpreters of poetry, not only of Holderlin's, incidentally.

Ten million can't be wrong, a hundred million even less so, with a billion it's out of the question.

What I'm getting at is: there would be no problem in getting ten million men and women to testify to the merits of whatever it is that is in need of promotion by any syndicate with the money and time to canvas them, but that wouldn't concern us, Melly (to whom I haven't yet come) and me, nor any of the patient readers who are still with us. There is nothing more irrelevant than consensus.

Last winter I went to stay with a doctor friend in Gstaad, Switzerland, and—an indication of my disturbed emotional and mental state— acted as though I was adept at winter sports.

I warned the reader—did I not?—that as well as being in the nature of a thesis, this narrative is also a self-survival manual with which all dwellers on the planet who ask for one should be supplied. But thirdly it is a private and intimate diary from which I now interpolate an exhilarating extract. But first a meditative passage.

What was I engaged on of a serious nature? Trying to keep some tenuous lines of communication open between myself—my consciousness—and reality. I'll list them: a fragile wooden container that might by now have crumbled to dust in a primitive dwelling in the Middle East, an amateurish interest in, and part-time study of, astro-physics, some sketchy conclusion about the nature of the molecular structure of the human brain, a study of the Old and New Testaments, not just as a scholar but as a believer, that's to say, with an open response to the claims and promises of the Gospel Jesus despite his prophecies and sense of solar time being far out. I even, both at hours of near-despair and of optimistic well-being, prayed to a favourite saint, something I could never have confessed to anyone.

By the time I entered the ski hut (hut, the fleeting association with another hut in another time and space flashed in a momentarily blinding implosion) I was a different person, one of my other selves, one I had never been before and hadn't known was a member of the cast. The attire accentuated the transformation as I thrust a foot into a heavy boot held by an executioner and the boot strapped onto the long runner, one of the doctor's spare pieces of equipment. And, hardly knowing what I was saying, I mentioned perfectly coolly and casually that my own gear had been left behind in Montreux. If, as I believe, possession by demons takes place, so also does infiltration via the subconscious by angelic influences.

I stood, muffled, gloved, a stick in each hand. Did I say a prayer? Yes and no. I recall the incident in the New Testament where the Devil tempted Jesus to cast himself from a tower, saying: It is written that His angels shall bear thee up.

Teetering on the edge of the snowy abyss I see, looking back, I could still have turned, and supported by the doctor, re-entered the hut. That was theoretically, had my normal faculties been at least partially operational, possible but of course they were not.

As in the crossing of all vital thresholds, psychic, emotional, physical (including I surmise that of death) it went unrecorded. Then I was in what I supposed was approaching the state of free fall, which astronauts experience, and Einstein researched, though this is of course speculation and probably erroneous.

I was making long transverse sweeps on the steep decline, possibly following by an inner automatic pilot the only viable route, or there may have been tracks visible. All I can recall, and that only when between sleep and waking, is that I thought I was experiencing what King David had when he danced before the Ark of the Lord.

I returned to the Middle East, but Joshua was dead. Still what inspired me were accounts of the early settlers flying illegally there with all those on board, excepting two old men crippled with arthritis and perhaps sciatica, standing up and reciting from the psalms of celebration as they crossed the Mediterranean coast.

From those early days of prayer and fasting, of life in a kibbutz and vigils at holy sites such as the one where Jehovah had commanded Abraham to sacrifice his son, Isaac —calling to mind the same Megiddo with which I had been deeply involved—there was a slow decline that accelerated as it continued.

One day there arrived in Tel Aviv film-makers in big black automobiles from Egypt, earlier of course from Hollywood, scattering combat boots, helmets, guns, bayonets and footprints in a location near the city.

This was in 1967—I think—and the film was shot, then edited in the US well in advance of the Israeli victory over the Arabs, after which it was screened in cinemas world-wide. Later, when Nasser died, after the abortive reconciliation attempted by President Nixon to help his re-election, the brilliance of the funeral outshone the sensation of his death, or so Joshua told me. The cradle, the football, call it the coffin, pitched and flew in the air and almost soared over the heads of the jubilant mourners. A great game, the ball went into the scrum and reappeared on another corner of the screen. (He had been speaking of the film, not the event itself, as I only then grasped.)

High time I introduced myself. That I have not, tells the reader a lot.

Lodsi Dormondi, Hungarian father, Irish mother. Also a few words more about Joshua. I don't think I have brought him up to date, put him in the immediate picture. The following details I got from his friend, Micaah.

He was, is, (I have not yet recorded his murder) a member of an extreme faction in, and outside, the Knesset. Outside, he has a band, brigade, armed, part bodyguard, but also vigilantes putting on occasional shows of power in the streets of Haifa, where they have a following, and Jerusalem where he often stays with Micaah at the King David Hotel.

Any proposition supported by a consensus can be dismissed. I interpolate these slogans to counteract the commercials, one of which I have just watched out of an inertia which it increased. Consensus is never history. Cleopatra and Mark Anthony on the Nile after the defeat of her fleet at the naval battle of Actium —that is the stuff of life-enhancing myth.

Anthony and the Queen of Egypt were extremists, fully committed to each other—"Let the wide arch of the ranged empire fall". Need I say, I am not Mark Anthony.

Still, I'm emotionally extravagant. I don't bargain, or keep open a way of retreat, as most of us do, but leave "most of us" out of it—as should be clear by now, this is not a social commentary. Yet I had a glimpse of what changes would have to take place down in my roots and was appalled. I recalled a smallish palm-like plant I had kept in a large pot and that had begun to sicken, frond by frond. I had unpotted it and found the threads of root closely squeezed together instead of reaching out into the plentiful mixture of soil, sand and peat. And this I took now as an image of my own psychic situation.

I had untangled and spread the roots and repotted the palm, but what an agonising intervention, to parallel that down in the quivering antennae of my own nervous system! As an escape or evasion, I planned an essay dealing with the prophets, both the ancient and the later ones.

There were times when I thought I would not have minded dying, evacuating space and exiting from time. A pity I hadn't broken my neck on the *piste*.

Of course this is a boast made to my secret and irresponsible self at one of the darker hours of desperation.

Wasn't I better off with Sabra in my suburban retreat — better, that is, than gadding about — despite the loneliness? And after the cat's death and before Sabrina came, despite an isolation that would have set in and turned the days into interminable, unendurable arctic winters and the nights dream-haunted and desperate, would it still not have been better?

That is what did it, the despair, the deconstruction. I needed to be brought to wishing myself cancelled and annulled before I could listen with sufficient detachment to see what was happening to me, or to see why it happened. Not because I was one of the latter prophets but because it required — who required? I'll come back to that if I, the narrator of this report, survive what is now to be ventured on — everything, all my experiences, inner and outward, from the Megiddo excavations, indeed much earlier, my marriage (which I have not yet reverted to), to studying Heidegger, by way of Wittgenstein, to my megalomania leading to not realising my restrictions in time and space, or (is this a relapse into *la folie des grandeurs?*) a shake-up of its molecular structure, itself based on atoms from the farthest constellations.

What were, are, the immediate effects? (Yes, I still cling to the question-and-answer style.) Not the cancelling of mortality, the dead stayed dead, and the living were still going to die, but death did not establish an impenetrable frontier between.

I don't much care for Martin Heidegger if anyone is interested (that's not quite true: I'm in awe of him), though I prefer him to most of his detractors. And here is the place to claim a personal, if indirect, interest.

We were in Freiburg-in-Breisgau, my late wife and I, at the end of World War II; to be factual we were brought there under military escort by two French soldiers from Bregenz prison across the Austrian frontier. That was in 1945. Later, on Bastille Day, we were freed from the villa in which we had been lodged while being interrogated (not Madeleine) somewhat cursorily by a sympathetic French (Alsatian) intelligence officer. It wasn't long before Madeleine had permission, which I took to include myself, to read in the university library, from where it was but a few steps to attending lectures in the philosophy department. With a very slight shift in chronology we might have heard Heidegger himself.

We were free, though having to report occasionally to the French police in Freiburg, where Heidegger had been banned from teaching on the arrival of the Allies a few months earlier. As it was, we heard a junior lecturer and former student of the Master deliver lectures either from Heidegger's notes or recordings—if such there were—of his scripts.

In 1951 he resumed his professorship but by then we had moved on to Paris.

I now return to the dead or, to put it more intuitively, *they* return as soon as a space, a clearing in the forest, as Heidegger would say, is made. In the end however he turned to art, to poetry and painting as the best, perhaps the only, way of our articulating our wonder and care (*Sorge*—I add the German word because it is precious in itself). Heidegger had a grasp of what poetry in particular was saying in its secret, but in a sense very ordinary, very much "at-hand" language. From Holderlin, Rilke, Stephan George, Celan, he concluded, among other things, that death was a vital part of Being but also that loneliness, that normally dull *angst* that waxes and wanes, comes from our shutting off of the dead.

(This is from my essay or thesis on the prophets, as is what immediately follows, including a poem, of which I occasionally write a few.)

I shall admit here that I don't understand all of this, and that both Holderlin and Celan even when read out, even by a woman, don't affect me in the way they do, not just Heidegger but many isolated, simple (simple that is in their immersion in the concrete, everyday world) souls. Yes, I use the word expressly because of its being totally out of fashion in academic and so-called enlightened circles ...

Into the Dark

Head inclined, the body can relax,
Cat on my knee, whiskey in my glass.
Messages? Send them by a thing called Fax.
Life is still worth the trouble and the pain.
News? There is Reuter, also Tass.
Friend or lover? Long outlived I fear,
Shall I re-meet the dear lost ones out there?
There is neither assurance nor idea.
Memories endure and these may well remain
Into the dark across the silent plain.

Our dead, those once close, with whom we banished loneliness, often indeed not yet knowing of its lurking presence, can, through us eliminating the gap or frontier that we make uncrossable without realising it, once more share intimately in our being.

Much of Rainer Maria Rilke's poetry is a life-long meditation on death and dialogue with the dead, carried on in the silent intervals between words as well as in tone, rhyme and rhythm. Because we are in a German situation I have been conducting this sketchy guide through German writers but of course it could be as well—in my case better—applied to poets in the English language such as Keats, Wordsworth, Christina Rosetti, Emily Bronte, and Robert Lowell.

Once M, my late wife and I, spent several days, or our leisure hours during them, pinning up reproductions of our favourite paintings, one of the multitude of memories that I recall most intensely as some of the happiest of a lifetime. Happy ... Happiest. I make use of the word though I know a little about its deceptive guises, its beguilements, its application to all sorts of, including ignoble, experiences. I and she experienced a sharing-caring that is the opposite to loneliness, an anti-loneliness such as we hope for and desire rather than are granted.

Apart that is from some lucky childhoods. Can the fully fledged and winged bird be whistled back to the nest, or even to the broken bough?

For me the answer is: I do not know. Maybe I know something, or have an intimation that I keep to myself outwardly. What does it come to? A shelf of photos in the sun parlour where I have dinner on summer evenings and which can be heated, if inadequately, in spring and summer (our autumns are mostly golden).

Mes souvenirs. A photo of Ferdinand Celine in Denmark soon after the last world war when he had been condemned to death by the French government of the time (now the bookshops display his writings and various critical works on them as well as several biographies). He is wearing a long, threadbare-looking coat and carrying a basket with a handle. Where is he off to? The gate at the end of the avenue to collect some fresh eggs, his post, the newspaper? A companion—has he such a one?—has just exclaimed: Hi! or Hey! or even *Ça va*! and he glances over his shoulder with a fugitive expression. Do I imagine this detail?

On the other side of the glossy page which I tore from the French illustrated paper, *Match*, is another photo, one of Edith Piaff in bed reading St Thérèse of Lisieux's *Story of a Soul.* There in the one frame, though both cannot be displayed simultaneously, are contemporaries of mine, so to say, whose associations link up with great psychic historic events, present and past.

Yes.... That powerful current joins, enters the smaller stream along which I was going, shortly before it had, not for the first time, occurred to me that Jesus had had not only the poor and lowly as followers but the well-to-do and well-regarded, mostly rich women. This is not stressed, hardly mentioned, by those who did the later reporting, sometimes from the accounts of eye witnesses, as if it did not fit in with their preconceived image, nor that of the prophets. The exception, the most significant anyhow, is St Paul who has little or no interest in the material conditions, the daily living style, of Jesus (and whose robust language did much to reverse the constant and natural emasculation of language, all language, through the wear and tear of popular usage).

Back to Heidegger, from whom once trapped it is hard to depart. Take him for a stroll along the Dreisam on a winter night in Freiburg, not in summer when it is only a trickle between boulders, but when the stars are bright. How many could he recognise? Would he have even stared upwards? Would Wittgenstein, come to that? That is why I loved Joshua. He took what was to hand and praised God and the Holy Spirit. He made wonderful use of what was to hand like the servant with the three talents. He found himself here as a semite and he devoted himself to Pan-Semitism. He stared down the wells that he had discovered and refreshed his vision. How long and passionately he would have looked through telescopes into the night of stars, had one been available! There was a war, rather limited, on his doorstep and he distinguished himself in it, though when he saw the manipulators filming it before it had taken place he was shocked and outraged. He lived his own complex innocence.

I take with wonder what is there and celebrate it, compose a litany to it. Heidegger didn't have to advise me on that. The creative spirit walked with Adam and Eve in the cool of the evening and they were astonished at what was all around them.

Joshua worshipped—in his own manner, pragmatic and trance-like at the same time—the God of Abraham, Isaac and Jacob, of the same triple name as the one that Pascal had stitched into his jacket or shirt. Did he—Joshua—also "believe in" the Gospel Jesus? Yes or no? Put like that I would answer: No, but that is always and ever the wrong way of asking. He had chosen me, not despite my being a Christian but because of it—in the tradition of St Paul.

He almost certainly had not read the Gospels, it would have gone against the grain of tradition. Had he done so, he would have been in for some shocks ("Before Abraham was, I am" and indeed the testimony of the women). While too many, or too searing, shocks can damage and deconstruct our beings, shocks are what keep those enquirers among us on course, the rockets firing when the initial impetus is declining.

The most violent shock, though finally salutary, from Heidegger is his postulate that our consciousness, or self-consciousness, is not the peak of human achievement. I have, or had, the idea that Being reached a high ground in an act of thought. But no. Thinking it over, I saw that an act of love was the highest ground. Something that as far as I make out, Heidegger does not suggest, which brings us to the region of his culpability in regard to his support of the German dictator and his barbarism. Brings me there, impels me to acknowledge the facts, but, of course, not to adopt the role of judge. A simple soul (simple in a worldly sense) would castigate him as one of the army of tormentors, in or out of uniform, the difference being uniforms are used to disguise the mass horrors, individual ones can be committed in plain attire.

Oh, besides the gravity of my unbalance I have gained some wisdom throughout a life such as I am not only doing a commentary but a dissertation on. And one of the chief, as well as most useful, of those insights is that a quarrel that in itself may be about nothing (we can't remember how it started) opens a fear or doubt in the mutual faith and care—Heideggers *sorge*—between the two and there is an opening for the powers and principalities of evil to flood in. Yes, I know of the presence of these powers in the outer darkness and of their threat, and cannot take comfort by being laughed at as a prey to superstition.

So I think of, brood about, Martin Heidegger and his apparent alliance—flirtation, at the least—with some of the more savage of these powers. Very briefly, as I was awakening the other morning, an explanation came to me, clear, clairvoyant. And then, before it registered on my memory, it flickered out. I had evidently dreamt it, which shows such an explanation exists, an explanation of how easily a fine mind can be open to invasion by these principalities.

There is a knock on my door (I'm imagining, but when am I not?) and the chief authority's *aide-de-camp*, or whoever would be entrusted with so delicate a mission, stands there. I ask him in.

Would I take on the post of supreme judge of an alternative judicial system with the powers of pronouncing the death penalty? In a flash I recall the unthinkable, the injuries inflicted on the badgers I read of—and briefly recorded—the other day.

I would consider it, consult two or three of those close to me and respond shortly.

How could I refuse? Oh, there are a lot of "decent folk" who will ask how could I *not* refuse. The firing squad—the one method of execution that need not be obscene and that I could watch if I had to (and I would feel an obligation if I had been the arbiter).

Speaking of arbiters, there was another knock on my door a few days later (there had of course been some between canvassers and collectors)—the supreme arbiter stood there. I shall return to this a little later. Now, read on.

I had a letter from Micaah. "Softly as an arrow of snow, the arrow of anguish fell." She wrote in bad German that two men had broken into the hotel room (not the King David) in Jerusalem where she and Joshua had been in bed and pierced his skull at the temple with several bullets. He had died within minutes, as she cradled his head in her arms, and whispered to him (this last she didn't write).

Loss ... yes, for me loss beyond any since the death of my loved ones, including the absence of Sabra from my daily and nightly existence, but to embark on a scale of measurement or comparison is utterly inappropriate.

The Pan-Semitic vision dispersed because I do not suppose anyone else knew of it, probably not even the girl.

I know someone, an acquaintance, not a friend, who had a truly loved cat and when it died soon bought another of the same breed (Persian) that looked identical and gave it the same name. That's one way of trying to deal with mortality, putting the clock back, reversing time, not only healing the wounds, but having plastic surgery applied to them so that there are no scars.

Dinosaurs dominated this earth for considerably longer than has man. No, I am not off into a fantasy orbit, I am reflecting on what it needs to take over the planet and concluding, not for the first time, that cats never could—not because they lack the bulk and strength of the dinosaur but because in our new phase what is needed is brain power, the kind of electro-magnetism inside the skull, an intelligence neither imaginative nor creative, nor the kind which is mysteriously present in original artists.

Here I want to make clear (that sounds like a politician starting to disavow all his opportunist twists-and-turns by announcing an undeviating principle) that any élite I may recognise has nothing to do with being a poet or painter. Outside that very circumscribed area are most of the courageous — in endurance — compassionate, companionable, comforters of the ostracised, human and animal.

—Yes, we had the kind of brain that could take over after the dinosaurs, but it isn't flexible enough to sustain a beneficial dominance. We're making an incredible mess of it, quite unbelievable to an average citizen of a hundred years ago. Pop culture, electronic entertainment, well and good — an earlier citizen would have, if horrified, accepted that, if painstakingly explained. Of where we are now, some of us, the vanguard, is endlessly gullible, asking no questions, announcing that all is well and if they follow the simple instructions, is going to get better and better.

What, at this moment, am I most in need of? A manual, a book of instructions on how to exist on this planet, a user's guide such as manufacturers issue with machines and technical equipment, but not the agency for human beings to its products.

So it has to be a "do-it-yourself" undertaking: I must compile my own user's manual for myself and any dependents, animals included.

Having described an execution by firing squad, or contemplated doing so (I have heard but not witnessed one), I shall now introduce a scenario of a sensual nature, to hang on the other side of the fireplace.

The unthinkable is always the most sensational, whether horrible or pleasurable. So I take it an exciting copulation takes place least expectantly. (Not that the expected and waited for love-making cannot compete.)

No .... I am not in the mood, physical, psychic, emotional, to embark on such an episode. However the time is sure to be ripe after a few days or weeks.

□□□

After advancing a bewildering number of reasons for composing this chronicle, none of which were satisfactory, I believe I have at last tripped over the main one which was right under my feet.

We wake up, come to consciousness, on this planet, confronted by all that is, which is to say the vast, awesome, incomprehensible and threatening cosmos.

When introduced to infinitely less daunting artefacts whose purpose and application is not immediately evident, there is an instruction leaflet, even booklet, provided.

Yes. This is a user's guide on how best to accommodate the complex and hyper-vulnerable human amalgam of nerves and neurons, flesh and blood, sperm and ovaries, to the experiences of a lifetime.

You may ask—though I doubt it—-is there not a built-in instinct that at least points in the least disastrous directions? In the case of animals this may be so, but there is no evidence of it in humans. What is more likely to be enquired about are my credentials. I have them ready and to hand.

They come from experience not postulates, from the desert and the wells, via Joshua, from underground (Megiddo), the ancient scriptures, the sight of the Ark that led to a glimpse of King David dancing before it, from Sabra, from the Psalms, from the Gospels, even from Heidegger.

What have I learnt, concluded, from all this? If I had to put it in one word, *compassion*, to be compassionate. Then, faith. Faith in what? In the historicity of the New Testament and quadruple recording of the short public life—two or three years—of Jesus. What reason, outside of my very subjective, ravaged, phenomenological state of mind, could be produced as independent evidence for this assumption?

The proviso "independent" is confusing. If it means evidence from other sources, other individuals—leave out organised groups—then there is much.

It is very difficult—arduous—to summarise how I entered by a side door so to say into the situation recorded by the four evangelists. This condition is a rare one I think, though again more of us may have fleeting experiences of it than is supposed.

I cross thresholds of feeling and intuition to an area where I am in a close accord with the life style—life and death style—obtaining in much of the Gospels and there taken for granted.

But now it is time to call a meeting of those who have stayed with me from the start, or, rather, hold a seminar in which readers have a chance of putting questions, making suggestions and formulating critiques of the whole enterprise.

It took place in my suburban bungalow—however, I'm not going to list the guests or students. Some left early, some came late, one or two who had walked out returned. Some never opened their mouths, others couldn't restrain themselves.

A tall dark individual, a man, jumped up, spread his arms and shouted (this was my impression).

—Am I a traitor? Do I look like one? Who dares call me a traitor because I haven't gone along with the mob of intellectual liberals? I didn't scream into the microphone at mass rallies. Fools are in the majority and that's a game they are sure to win. I've never signed any manifestos, not even for the victims. If I am victimised by my own people, nobody is going to bemoan my fate ...

I called him to order, though it is something I never did in my life before, reminding him that this was a semi-private seminar, not a public meeting. Sabrina was on my lap.

—To study two great prophets, divided by several millennia, David, King of Israel, who danced before the Ark of the Covenant and Martin Heidegger.

—What about Ernest Bloch, enquired Nadezhda, a very old woman who touchingly had made what was for her the perilous journey from the other side of the city by train.

—Let's not stray too far.

I was going to keep control of the proceedings, not a role I relish.

—An interesting question, Nadya, and thank you for being here, but we shall have to limit ourselves to ...

I am not going to be bogged down in my own part in the seminar, because its purpose is to attempt to transform a narrative—a dissertation—in which the author (or authority) writes and his audience read, as passively as television watchers, into a discussion. At first thought this appears impossible, but let us try.

To start with, the suggestions, opinions and questions of those present should be read aloud, in the spirit of Heidegger, the initial subject of the event. The importance of a proposition can best be judged by the language in which it is proposed and language communicates most flexibly, dialectively, in spoken words.

Have I managed to get any of my readers to come along? How can I tell unless they proclaim themselves, as one couple, introducing themselves as Georg and Marthe Fussenegger from Austria do.

—We're from Dornbirn (I hadn't heard of it, a village not all that far from where we were and in turn less than a hundred kilometres from Messkirch in the Black Forest where, as you may be aware by now, Heidegger was born and died. These proximities, by the way, though spanning three countries, gave me some reassurance).

—We have read the Professor's treatise about archeology and the Old Testament, announced a student—as well as his fictional, or perhaps factual, account of the life and times of a cat called Sophie. I don't think I mentioned that she was Sabra's mother (my own aside).

—Is that the one? a man, presumably her husband, enquired, pointing to Sabrina.

—A mind immersed for a long lifetime in meditation and astonishment is, whatever besides, not a mediocre or trivial one. (Another *non sequitur* to add to all the others that further disrupt this journal.)

Who came up with this, but let it go for the moment while the sense of death gains momentum.

I had drawn at least two readers out of the anonymity of that small but scattered band, and an unlikely couple at that. But that gave me an inkling that, outside those of my friends who responded positively to what I write, and not all of them do, the majority could value it for what I didn't know was there.

—*We* know, Lodsi, Marthe Fussenegger is telling me—you see I have a married sister up in the Black Forest not far from Messkirch. Last year I spent a holiday in a hotel at Titisee and the prophet, or Herr Professor, as the manager called him, used sometimes to drive over for dinner. Of course that was a long time ago, what, thirty years perhaps, and Herr Schulberg was an old fellow with a grey beard. He still supervised the kitchen, prepared some special dishes himself, so I said, cook us—that is, me and the boy, the baby too was with me but Georg had been too busy to leave Dornbirn (what can occupy somebody in a place so obscure that nobody I asked ever heard of it?).

I didn't hear the end of the tale because of a student, who may have thought I was being unduly monopolised, and so interrupted with a question.

There was a lot of banter going on at the other end of the room, to which I quickly put a stop. Yes, I can induce awe. That may come as a surprise to you who have conscientiously read these diary entries so far. The last incidentally is dated May 21, 19—

To return to the question that one of the mature women asked me: Did I agree that television commercials, though still in their crude infancy, were already replacing the visual arts and even some of the other ones, and largely because they focussed on some of our most obsessive aspirations like the overcoming of the limitations of time and space? For instance, they promoted the cult of the motor car which had turned an age-old dream into everyday experience, if only to a somewhat limited extent ...

Did I what? If I haven't made this crystal clear, then what have I done?

By now I had given up the plan of concluding the seminar by gathering up all the loose pieces and fitting them together in a grand mosaic of my own design; what I was assembling instead were my resolution and nervous energy to have the room cleared (and later cleaned and restored to its normal arrangement).

What I longed for, hardly aware of it, was an ordinary, very ordinary (if such exists) marriage — doing the weekly shopping together, perhaps with a family car, perhaps making the most of taxis, sleeping in the same bed, with sex never quite out of our heads, night or afternoon, but with a feeling of more than indifference, even a willed forgetfulness, of the name Martin Heidegger, so that when I happened to see it on the spine of a book in our modest library it didn't cause any vivid or disturbing recollections. On the contrary I might feel a fleeting loss, as an adult when some object recalls an exciting childhood game, and he or she smiles, not in superiority, no, but with a faint nostalgia.

I long for a tranquil habitat where on a quiet evening a bell from a distant church could be heard faintly tolling. I pored over maps, imagining that we were among the luckiest couples in the world, free to choose where we would make our home, knowing our relationship was steadfast, envisaging the lighter moments of companionship such as discussing what we would have to start the day which those who haven't known years of lonely breakfasts, as I have, will perhaps not fully grasp the healing grace bestowed thereby.

Is such mature bliss, as distinct from the fleeting euphoria of youth, possible on this planet? No, or I think only when the end —reality, death—is concretely present. Maybe for those stricken by a terminal affliction.

Poland, that's a land that appeals to me. I've a friend with a sister there. We wouldn't settle in a city but near enough to one of the smaller ones to do our weekly shopping there by car, as I think I've noted.

One of the other aspects of all this is very funny, even if not comic enough to lead to a good belly laugh. The response to sex of an uninterested citizen committed to moral values but often with a deep-frozen heart in his or her breast, is shock and disgust.

To sum up, a rather pretentious exercise in this situation, the most effective compensation for the majority of humans in this harsh world, making it tolerable for many, are the joys of coupling.

It is time, high time, I imagine, for the Fusseneggers, who have become the touchstone for normality and common sense as I compose this Song of Songs and, at times, Dirge of Dirges, to have their say.

Let us move on, not gradually and smoothly which, as I may have noted repetitiously, nature never does, but in a small swift leap with no trace of transition.

It is time I take stock, submit myself to the grand arbiter, although in his long, stained, torn overcoat and habitual forage cap he looked far from elegant, but obscurely impressive, yes.

GA: Tell me, apart from the care of cats and a general rapport with the animal kingdom, what have you mastered?

L: The art of succumbing to pain, to the very brink of despair, of teetering on the edge of the pit and then regaining balance just in time. And also, in the absence of actual tragedy, an imaginative skill and tendency to evoke, and dream, agonies of the more subtle and haunting kind.

GA: I'm listening. What else?

L: I grasp instinctively and in the way kinspeople grasp, without necessarily liking each other, the cosmos and its functioning.

GA: Have you a comparable understanding of close human relationships?

L: No, Your Excellency.

GA: Is Jesus the Son of God?

L: Undoubtedly.

GA: No doubts?

L: Nothing but doubts.

GA: To whom have you been a comfort besides Sabra?

L: Sabrina, the other cat.

□□□

Since adolescence when I used to fantasise that an old doubled-up mattress was the girl in Tolstoy's *Resurrection,* and thrusting deep into its musty folds experience a fever and excitement I've seldom had since during the real thing, I've almost never given myself an orgasm. It is sterile and a negation, or, because to assert or make statements on important issues is an error, one should simply question (which, incidentally, is the difference between the style of two famous physicists, Fred Hoyle and Stephen Hawkings), I'll ask is not masturbating a sad and desperate expedient?

I made a friend the other day. What first drew my attention to the old fellow was his shopping basket at the check-out, about the contents of which there was a brief exchange between him and the check-out girl.

He took out one of the items and explained in an accent quite different to the indigenous one (I learnt later it was upper-class English) that he had included it by mistake. It appeared to be a slice of meat wrapped and fastened with the red tape used in the store. None of the several tins of cat food were discarded.

—A foreigner too, I take it, he said to me on the way out.

My English or *Mitteleuropean* accent had been noticed as not being perfect, perhaps a long way short (one is unaware of one's own linguistic failings, or at least I am).

We exchanged introductions, mine had obviously no particular association for him, nor did his, Arthur Dewhurst, for me. Having come with me to my parked car, he lingered beside it while I stowed my purchases in the boot, although he had nothing much to say. He was, I thought, lonely, a condition I know quite a bit about. After some hesitation, by no means on the spur of the moment, I invited him round to my suburban abode the following evening and, his rather frozen expression melting momentarily, he accepted, or so I took his nod to indicate.

Still, I wasn't really expecting him when the next evening punctually at six there was a knock on my yellow front door.

There he was, gaunt, looking as if he expected to be turned away having knocked on the wrong door—the house isn't numbered as is common here.

I brought him in, fearing the invitation had been a mistake.

I had drinks at hand, a steadfast standby in such situations, and I was dreading my visitor announcing he didn't drink alcohol.

However, when I offered him a glass of wine he nodded, as I thought he would also have, had the suggestion been the Scotch whiskey, a bottle of which was also on the table.

His story was gradually revealed. Ah, how pitiable are these personal stories that are either our hidden, and sometimes only, treasure, or else torments; or, again, as with Arthur, a mixture of both. Yes, bereft of our stories what would we be, nobodies, nothing. We would still have our dreams, but would we—are not our stories and our dreams complementary?

He was accused in his native land of being a war criminal.

—I gave comfort to my country's enemies, he told me. That's the charge. But they weren't mine, certainly not all of them. I had more hateful private ones.

I waited. He said nothing more for several minutes—though that may be an over-estimate—and it didn't seem that I should put a question. Then he went on:

—I wrote and published an essay in a newspaper. It was a simple enough rational proposition, pointing out the ridiculous connotations in the recently coined phrase "war-crimes". These words in conjunction form a tautology, each denoting the same thing, because every act done in the furtherance of war, indeed every word pronounced for the same purpose, is a crime.

Had he put his argument as a question I would have been whole-heartedly in accord, but I distrust assertions, especially when made with such apparent self-confidence.

—Then you're a totalitarian pacifist, are you not, a turn-the-other-cheek-er? I asked.

—I don't think of myself like that, Mr Dormondi (he had used the name only once). You see, I'm not so utterly against violence when it is not official, uniformed, self-justifying violence. Between minor violence and hypocrisy, I will take the violence, a hot-blooded act, very possibly regretted as soon as done, whereas adopting an ethical stance to justify violence, posing as Christian, or whatever values are in vogue, crusaders infiltrates another lie into the litany of major lies which many find so comforting.

Fussenegger: "If widespread atrocities are being perpetrated against a helpless minority by a powerful nation, should not any sufficiently powerful outside groups or nations interfere? Don't answer theoretically, but as if you had a loved one either tormented and killed or among the gravely threatened."

I would say: Yes, they must. At the same time I know, and history confirms, that in the course of the intervention and, indeed, probably the more successful it is, atrocities, if of a different kind, are inevitably committed.

As he was leaving, Arthur somewhat surprised me by inviting me to visit him one evening the next week.

He had a bed-sitter on the ground floor of a house in a run-down district, though, for all I knew, it could be on the way up. The window looked onto a small overgrown back garden and was partly open which I took as an indication of the presence of the cat whose tinned food I had noticed in the shopping basket but to which the old fellow had not referred.

I have not an eagle eye, not for what doesn't vitally concern me, such as the interiors of the dwellings of friends and acquaintances, but the place was tidy and there was a small earthenware pot of primulas on the only table. I must have mentioned a display of just such small pots of flowers outside a shop in all weathers round the corner from me, and had the sentimental thought of which I'm not ashamed, that the faces of the flowers that always seemed turned to the wind were waiting to find a sheltered home. Had the same idea impelled Arthur to spend what may well have been for him a not negligible amount?

On this occasion I kept the conversation off such general topics as violence, war and peace, the state of the world. This was easy as Arthur was not much of a conversationalist and it was up to me to do most of the talking. When I came to a stop, he was silent with his head in his hands, but without any sense of awkwardness or strain being generated. Indeed, it was then that I realised there was a tranquility here such as is rare in human habitations.

I shall not try to record my impressions and his "sayings" in precise sequence. It is best, I think, to list his propositions into one small collection, his unveiling of his career and his unbaring of his heart into separate passages, though they all overlapped.

He had started World War II as a lieutenant-general, one of the youngest in the British army, and a recognised tactician of tank strategy, had earlier met his opposite number in the

Wehrmacht, Guderian, had been a friend of Basil Liddle-Hart's and, after the war, of his son Adrian.

As I've mentioned, he was scathing about the reinvocation of the concept "war crimes", seeing it as an indirect justification for the waging of "non-criminal" wars.

He had been a prisoner, took part in the mass escape from the prison camp for officers in Silesia in the mid-forties, but instead of joining the others in an attempt to return to the UK via the Baltic or however, had been sheltered in their farm house in Pomerania, by an east German family until 1946 when he had managed to travel to Ireland and obtain a residence visa on the strength of a grandmother from County Cork.

These years in Pomerania were the most valuable, he told me, in his life. Living on the slope of a volcano, though not perhaps a very threatening one, he had been granted (that is how he put it) the insights that had sustained him since.

I was enjoying myself in an obscure manner, obscure to me, though I realised it was harmless compared to the involuntary pleasure that at times comes from hearing of the setbacks and discomfortures of acquaintances. The old fellow struck me as a hero of a kind rare these days, such as I particularly admired.

Then came the incident of the cat which so far hadn't appeared. It is an event small in itself as all events connected with these creatures must be in the panorama of world happenings, and I shall only sketch the outlines, sparing readers who are not cat lovers, or indeed heartily sick of them by now. I have readers in both of these categories and no less faithful for that, whereas those readers who question or dismiss my ventures into the unchartered, cosmological or religious, are temperamentally alien.

The cat was black with a long, though not Persian, unhealthy coat, standing up or "staring" as I've heard it called. She jumped onto the sill of the open window and sat there while Arthur called her in.

—She's shy of strangers.

Yes and no. Take my word for it, it was not of me, or not only me, of whom the creature was wary. Arthur got up, I think somewhat embarrassed, and went towards the window, but before he reached it the cat had fled, and that is the correct word to denote her vanishing.

Could the small beam that this incident threw on Arthur Dewhurst's persona cancel out the number of admirable attributes I had appraised and stored at the back of my mind? Yes, it did, rightly or wrongly, and which I cannot be sure.

◻◻◻

Yes, I was lonely, when hadn't I been, but I won't go into that. Striking up an acquaintanceship with the first, second, or third male shopper at the local store was not of course an inspired way to mitigate the condition.

What about women? Three-and-a-half had signalled, albeit from afar, that they were available. For what? That would be left to evolve in its own private manner, we weren't in a bordello. I say three-and-a-half because the gossamer web the fourth had spun—if I hadn't imagined it—had a loophole in it, and indeed may have been nearly all loophole, as the latest fashion in cosmology is to postulate not just the existence of Black Holes (*déjà vu* or *non-vu*) but the universe itself as a singularity or gigantic Black Hole.

To bring this intimate diary right up to date I'll quote the last entry, dated April 28, "on my way to the races".

Before the last of the six races I was in the basement under the main stand where the totalisator operates, watching, with no intense interest, the fluctuating prices electronically flickering against the numbers of the half-dozen or so horses in the race.

On the course it was getting dark, the ground littered with discarded betting tickets and slips, but down here the naked bulbs shed a harsh light. There weren't a lot of people there, mostly, I suppose, the hard-core punters, sometimes known as "the talent", hoping to "get out" or recoup their losses on the final contest.

I took a man next to me, who never moved his gaze from the tote indicator board, to be one of these. As he moved away to the selling *guichets*—on the opposite side of the row to those that paid out—I moved too, but at a distance which did not—there seemed not to be many gamblers at this last-ditch encounter with fate—look as if I was following him.

The upshot: behind him at the *guichet* I saw him push a wad of notes—not rainbow-coloured like Dmitri Karamazov's, let alone blood-stained — and with them the number of a horse, or rather a six-year-old mare—as I saw from my race-card—that had remained favourite at 2-1 and 7-4 as long as we had been watching the state of the market.

I am describing the scene in some detail, but what I cannot do—music might be here a better medium, evoking the atmosphere of desperation—is enter into the world of the gambler. This glimpse though was enough to fascinate and also disturb me and my self-care in this regard and, half-magically (chemically?) to ensure he and I exchanging a few words and our telephone numbers.

Did the mare win? Yes, though that is largely incidental.

The old question, the same as ever, what was I doing there? What was I doing at any moment anywhere, come to that?

Looking back, I can see how the numerous worlds that I was led to, drifted into or, as at present, entered of my own volition, link up and form a fairly complex model of the—of course far more complex—real me, if such exists.

I shall list them in an attempt at a less befogged and negative attitude.

Megiddo, the stone dwelling in Transjordania, the monastery on the slopes of Sinai (which I may not have mentioned), the suburban interlude with Sabra and then Sabrina, and before that, Sophie.

Here is a psalm I often recite:

> *To Thee I lift up my spirit.*
> *My God I put my trust in Thee*
> *I shall not be let down*
> *Nor shall my enemies mock me*
> *For all those who wait on Thee*
> *Are not destined to disappointment.*
> *Lord, show me Thy way*
> *And teach me Thy paths.*

Horse racing. Here is part of an essay on the jockey, Smirke, I wrote.

Smirke had won four Derbys, the last on *Hard Ridden* (1959).

It was an area, very small and specialist, unknown to me, that I took to. I'm speaking about horse-racing, no other sport and not sport in general. Limited in extent, I soon saw it was a closed circuit of extraordinary subtleties. Biology, anatomy, a dexterity in garnering relevant data from very small time factors, and much else were part of making a success out of it. I'm not thinking of wagering, that's another story though closely linked, but of breeders, trainers and jockeys. Which brings me back to where I started. Charlie Smirke had died the previous year in his eighties.

Oh yes, a large percentage of the population in Europe, North America, Australia, South Africa, Dubai and some unexpected pockets where racing was followed on television had not only heard of—probably more than half knew the name—but were well versed in the details of a sensational career. I am speaking of really huge numbers, far beyond those who had ever heard of Wittgenstein or Heidegger, probably more than those who responded to the name of Einstein.

I'll terminate this preamble and take a sideways step or short leap—at which by now I am deft — to being invited to dinner by Smirke at his house near Epsom, though not—as the media had it—within sounds of the roar of the crowd.

I need not go into what was served, a relief as I wasn't taking the dishes in with precision. Smirke ate almost nothing, a small shrimp cocktail—the plumpest, fleshiest I ever tasted, but then Dublin Bay prawns are noted for being of a particularly fleshy kind, ironic seeing that flesh was what the jockey was eschewing.

So far I have failed to evoke this alternative world of racing in a manner accessible to, say, the Fusseneggers who never saw a thoroughbred horse in their lives. These are inlets in the formidable frontiers as I am about to indicate.

It is, of course, at its most obsessive and intense, an imaginary one but so set about, controlled and down to earth, to the actual sod — its firmness, softness, spring and texture — that it has most of the lineaments of what we are accustomed as the real and the imposed (as much of Heidegger's Being as the rest of what is).

What was the great jockey riding?

A colt of Prince Khaled bin Abdullah, to give him his native credentials, whose horses, divided over several trainers, must easily represent the most valuable single owner's bloodstock, that is and was through the winter a short-priced favourite for the race—called *Nothing Venture*, a smallish, dark bay colt by the American sire *Danzig* out of a mare closely related to the great Canadian sire, *Northern Dancer*. He will next be ridden by Prince Khaled's retained jockey, whose name he doesn't wish me to mention. It is world-famous.

The world of horse racing is an alternative world, a microcosm opposed to the consumer world that has taken over.

What is the true situation? Lies, semi-lies, prevarications: language or jargon is current in which lies are no longer lies because the threshold between truth and falsity has been shifted ...

For those without a historic sense (most of end of twentieth-century mankind) no alternatives are dreamt of ...

It is the age of packaging, of wrapping over wrapping. In days gone by it was only at Christmas or at children's birthdays that presents were so got up, and then for the suspense and excitement of opening them. Now, buy almost any commodity in a store or supermarket and it will be packaged in such a way as if the length of time taken in extracting the object is part of its intrinsic value.

Take razor blades, of which in self-service stores there is a bewildering display. Sets of these are clamped to a stiff piece of cardboard, the whole in a semi-transparent covering or envelope that could well have been designed to withstand a shredding machine (as used, I believe, for discarded, top-secret documents), out of which it would come with only slight defacement, if it did not clog the apparatus.

Another alternative is the garden: "Through what wild centuries roves back the rose?"

Do I communicate with the plants or they with me? No, though I have no reason to reject the possibility as sentiment, wishful thinking or a belief in their heightened sensitivity by those who claim they do.

Gardening is said to be a peaceful occupation and so it is if you bring your peace to it. There is little or no sensationalism in what is native to gardens which I consider of vital importance.

There is, however, a less than tranquil sight: the black cat that I had noticed previously a few times and occasionally place an enamel plate of cat food on the grass for when Catty was having her evening meal.

There it was, nameless, homeless, anonymous, waiting ... Waiting, as nothing else was, waiting without, I think, being conscious of doing so. Ah, how much I know about waiting and how well I know it in all its subtle manifestations. Will the phone ring, will there be a faint, or not so faint, clang of the door knocker, a beloved voice at long (perhaps only an hour's duration) last calling? Not that the black cat likely added the half-hope, half-despair of expectation to its misery. Her long black coat seemed to be ruffled in all directions, "staring" is again the word I think, and also wet, although I had inadvertently left the tool shed open. My little ditty was prophetic: "Take the cat to the vet." Yes, but how catch her?

There were the gnats (I've mentioned them, have I not?) at the same gyrations of their aerial dance as when I had watched them in the shade of the tall laurel bushes. What memories they brought back from the rich store from which without my knowing, some must have fallen out of the net that catches and stores the accumulation of the past. I was once upon a time standing at the bedroom window of a hotel in Luxembourg that looked out upon the deep gorge that divides the small city. Their slow, or is it swift, interlacings and circlings were as they had been for millennia.

They might have taken over when after their millions of years of dominance the dinosaurs vanished. The gnats could have danced their way above the humid swamps into their kingdom.

How does that correlate with the popular assumption that the planet is conditioned by chance or design (the distinction itself is open to question) for the ultimate emergence of the complexities and self-consciousness existing in the human brain and psyche, or nervous set-up? It doesn't. But if the coming into being of mankind means the agonies of various degrees that thinking-feeling entails, then who would choose this destiny?

Are you saying in your round-about way that you would return your entrance ticket to the show if you could locate the *guichet* where it wasn't so much purchased as thrust at you? I don't say that, but I don't set myself against saying it.

Should I start on a 'Short Treatise on Gnats'? I considered the project, but then started gardening, at first weeding, a tedious chore as I had supposed, but with its own satisfactions as in hand-weeding, when with a firm grip on the stalk a deeply spread root is extracted from the soil intact. Eliminate them, yes, but they too are worthy of a handbook. 'A Short Guide to Common Weeds'. Why short? Because all serious experts include the word in their learned dissertations: 'A Short History of Time', 'A Short History of English Literature' (from which Lord preserve us), 'A Short History of Women's Fashion', profusely illustrated.

However, all I did so far as writing is concerned is, as you see, continue with this record, together with the occasional poem:

> *I went by your gate but didn't come in,*
> *I think you are past redeeming,*
> *Devoured by an ego of black, black sin,*
> *Condemned, if you get my meaning.*
> *However, I'm not the final tribunal*
> *And at the heel of the hunt, at your funeral,*
> *A whisper at the graveside heard only by me*
> *Would plead for compassion, reporting that he*
> *Sheltered some furry and homeless beasts*
> *Keeping one of them constantly on his knee.*

Am I progressing, in my inner self and therefore in this narration? Evolving, I mean. Have the losses, one grievous, the strains and stresses, the failures, shameful at times, the indulged trivialities, worked together for my good? I don't know and who can tell me?

The Gospels relate that Nicodemus, a distinguished and revered Pharisee, came to Jesus by night. Yes ... but why, to discover what? Whether he was indeed the Messiah? I don't imagine so. Not to *ask*, to absorb and assimilate.

In any case, nothing important can be discussed directly. There are parables. Some use horse racing jargon as parable.

I am finding out that gardening can be a parable, and weeding a purging, a purgation. The pruning and spraying of rose bushes with fungicide which garden manuals devote much space to is not for me much to do with the garden. I say "the garden" trying to recall several gardens that have been there where I was at different periods, often at the periphery, but occasionally, as the one in which Sabra is buried, at the very centre.

Those who at the word "garden" see roses are probably the same people who at the mention of music envisage Mozart.

Yes, I'm aware that all this is getting us nowhere. Indeed, it has become so distasteful to me to jot down these trivialities that I am about to take the plunge, the leap without parachute or safety net that I have been so vainly postponing.

I started addressing myself:

—It seems to me, Lodsi, that you have spent most of your life in a rather desperate search for the treasure that would make it all worth-while. If you are convinced in the end that there is no pearl of great price buried in the field next door, then you don't want anything more to do with it, not only not with the heartbreak and anguish that nobody has put on record more movingly (what a boaster!), but also with the pleasures and excitements that keep a lot of people in different states of sedation up to quiet or violent desperation.

This isn't a lecture, however I make it sound.

Are the Fusseneggers still there, in their Black Forest abode?

There was a film, I didn't see it: *All This and Heaven Too*, and the "too" suggests that all this life is, or can be at moments, a foretaste of heaven, doesn't it?

"I could do with a gin-and-tonic" (diary entry).

"Should I be attired in sackcloth and ashes?" (*ibid*)

I am not rejecting what is here, things as they are, but trying to understand them. We aren't demanding, or begging, for miracles or even dispensations, not for the old rewards: eternal beatitude, reunion with the lost ones. It seems to me, though I haven't yet got round to meditating on this, that our first concern is that the great events, experiences, that illuminate the outer chaos, revealing for a moment a harmony, taking place in obscurity, burning themselves out in an intensity of love and compassion, are preserved. That is that they should not pass and perish and that those who seek this assurance are given it, in however fragile and with whatever contradicting asides, for only the pure in heart, if not in the mortal flesh, can clearly decode such signals.

—Wonderful! (Is this the Fusseneggers?)

June 20 (Diary)

Because what I call this diary is subject to long intermissions that can extend to a number of years, there will be drastic changes to place, situation, psychic and physical, in consecutive passages.

This has both a good and a bad side, beneficial because it extends the circle of the trawl and both more and more varied fish (events) are captured.

If I head the entries, or some, with a monthly date, but not the year, it is merely to keep an awareness, in my and the reader's mind, of the form I have chosen and so indulge in flexibility without excuse.

Here we are, then, in the living room of my suburban bungalow, detached and set in trees. In one corner is a small table on which there is a Byzantine icon of Virgin and Child, a photograph of St Thérèse of Lisieux as a postulant in Carmel, her immature face already puffy with the symptoms of tuberculosis, and a votive lamp that is sometimes lit and sometimes not. That is to say it is not lit when I am expecting a woman to call about whom I compose sexual fantasies, and even without any such expectation it is often unlit out of laziness and neglect.

All this has its shameful aspect or is simply shameful and despicable.

Now I shall pass on to another passage included in the diary, an essay on TV commercials or rather a fake or send-up commercial, featuring all the essential characteristics.

It can start with a neatly but not smartly attired middle-aged, middle-class gentleman with a moustache looking you (the camera) in the eye and recounting how he recently suffered a heart attack which, though recovered from, has left him without a job. Providentially he was insured with the X Life Assurance company and so can put all financial worries behind him and "get on with and enjoy the business of living".

"Well," I hear the Fussenegers say—good, thrifty folk—"nothing wrong with that, is there?" And not only the imaginary couple from the Black Forest but some very actual and much respected men and women, such as a large proportion of the spectators of Wimbledon who, as I read, are always behind a losing champion, never willing on the challenger who they see as tainted with some kind of unspecified subversion.

Let's get on with the mock TV commercial. Washing powder, motor cars and a flaky, crisp cereal are the most frequently advertised commodities, because evidently most profitable.

"If we can't convince the buggers that the peak of felicity equates with riding in our brand of automobile, attired in a gleaming white shirt and with a packet of flakes handy, by friendly persuasion, then we'll prise the money out of them by Goddamn fear (uninsured heart attacks, break-ins and cold fevers, anything that takes their minds, or what passes for such, off football and sex)."

The grand finale: when the World Cup is finally won, it is borne aloft into the TV studios and, when placed on the table-altar between two lit candelabra, is seen to be full of the noxious cereal.

What inspires or gives me any right to act the scourging prophet in the tradition of Isaiah, Daniel, Ezekiel? The question is academic, because as so much of this narrative-diary has been about, it is presenting my credentials. I, Lodsi Dormondi, of mixed parentage, confused, patient, compassionate and far from innocent, though venerating the innocent above all, step into the breach (in default of anyone else in the vicinity doing so) in defence of whatever hasn't been smothered under the corn flakes.

There came through my letterbox with the usual consignment of consumer leaflets, appeals, proposals (for insurance, mortgages, et cetera) a discreet reminder that a doctor had moved into the neighbourhood. Another was from an advertising agency—presumably one of many meant for delivery to a business area—saying that they would handle the publicity and marketing of any commodity my firm wished to promote.

Believing as I'm sure is clear by now that imagination can extend actuality into reality—there is a connection here between Joshua's well-gazing, the cat's funeral and, yes, David's dance before the Ark — I composed in my head what I imagined would be the script of the medico's document. This was, as I say, an attempt to accelerate the actuality of the consumer into reality, into its proper perspective within the present life style on earth. Here goes then.

The doctor would skilfully and conscientiously (he was a non-drinker, non-smoker) perform all the tasks of a general practitioner, surgeon, forensic specialist and transplanter of organs, including autopsies, limb removals and skin grafts.

Returning to the advertising agency, they would publicise (all over the Common Market) any product my firm produced whose name and nature I entrusted to them.

Did I have such a commodity? You bet I did, in my head of course. I could hardly wait to get in touch with them. What was my treasure?

'Sea Soap', made of seaweed, including kelp, rendered down when fresh off the rocks into a dark, tangy substance which when applied to skin penetrated between the derm and epiderm—after all we came from amphibians—to refresh, and perhaps renew, withered and burnt-out tissue.

I am abandoning this confessional narrative and starting afresh.

A faithful reader: Bravo!

The Fussenegger couple (quintet by now for they have another infant): You can't. You'd betray our trust?

But I have, started from scratch I mean, with a protagonist in his seventies — Lodsi himself in later, saner years, who, retired finally to the South, grows dates, figs, a few olives in a river-bank orchard.

The reality is, however, that I fled to the jungle.

We go ahead with this crazy project which I can't even envisage at all accurately. Nobody half-way sane dreams of such fantasies, not to speak of operating them. But we are among the company afflicted with psychic malaise, those with whom Christ chose to associate, more than associate often, to love. Those, indeed, out of whom, like Mary Magdalene, seven devils were expelled. Oh, I know that very soon biblical scholars were referring to these as evil spirits in a moral sense. But at the time there was no such assessment. It was the psychiatric language of the time and place and considerably more to the point than our present jargon.

Nente. I have come to love and revere the name. Back to Orla and whom I called "Min", black-violet jolie-laide and with whom I made love. It is the first time in I don't know how long.

The holy memories, the sacred graves! But if they decompose, de-intensify there, and finally blend into the indifferent mould— then, are we not mocked and betrayed? But in the jungle I didn't ask this question.

—Has nobody done this before, do you suppose?

—What?

—Revert to the wild?

—Of course they have, thousands, tens of thousands, only it's usually in private.

□□□

I was almost young again.

When King David reached an advanced old age and could not keep himself warm, they sent lookers for a beautiful maiden throughout all the territory of Israel, and finally found Abishag the Shunamite and brought her to the king (First Book of Kings, Ch 1).

I needed nothing like this.

Afterwards they brought other girls, among them one called Micaah who may well have had a dream in which part of the future was revealed to her. This is not stated in the Old Testament, not to mention in the Pentateuch, there is no factual or historic evidence for it, but just as in the other area, eleven dimensions bring what is missing to the eternal harmony, so the communication that I am crediting Micaah with receiving in a dream—and this was a recognised way of imparting divine messages at the time—ties up, unifies, some loose strands in this narrative.

Joshua's Micaah, I could say my Micaah who is living in Haifa, shared the secret of the survival of the Ark of the Covenant with Joshua and myself. No doubt when King David, recalling perhaps his great sins, fell into depression and near-despair, his Micaah recalled the Ark which Jehovah had given him—and through him, the Israelites as a covenant.

In Jerusalem there were intrigues, plottings, and violence over who should succeed to the throne after King David's death. There were robbers and gangs, each with their candidate, several of whom came from outside Judaea. Had one of these been successful the whole sacred history, the lineage from David to Jesus as recorded in Mark, would have been broken.

There was no man-woman kissing in Nente and it had no part in the sensuality of ancient Israel, nor, come to that, in the New Testament, where it is an expression of compassion, loving kindness or veneration—that is how I kissed Orla.

A quasar shines with a brilliance, so those in the know proclaim, three hundred trillion times that of the sun. Does that put you in the picture?

It is a picture the jungle has always been aware of.

Mr and Mrs Fussenegger: We swallowed the Ark though it stuck in our throats, the jungle would choke us.

No, you, dedicated readers, won't see it pictured anywhere but here. It does not cross the thresholds of the media and so for many fails to become "real". Instead, on the blue television screen, the appeals in the commercials are screaming to the consumer to phone na-ow, na-ow, na-ow, knowing, if nothing else, that if he/she doesn't na-ow, they never will.

Yes, as there is poetry for certain kinds of communication, trigonometry for others, the song of birds for still more, so there may be the language of outward darkness and zero temperature. The particle cannot be captured in the same language in which travellers share their impressions, or still less, nurses comfort their patients in, not to as much as mention the way I establish contact with my cats.

We are here to "tend the miracle", by which I mean treasure what is given, including the pain, providing it doesn't, as with Melly (whom we'll shortly meet), exceed our nervous and mental endurance.

❏❏❏

Disaster ... inner devastation! Sabrina, Sabra's successor, is missing, lost, dead, stolen? Not since ... No, comparisons with earlier tragedies are irrelevant.

Why didn't I put a collar with my phone number on her? Because I feared she could get caught by a branch in a hedge. A prey to imaginary events of the far-fetched kind. One thing: she wouldn't stray. Run over? She—as far as I knew—never ventured out the front gate. And there would be the body retrieved by a neighbour, a limp rag of pale damp fur.

October 2

I didn't know miracles could be evil, oh, I didn't know the extent of the imaginative genius of the controller and regulator of events to inflict supreme and unpredictable agony on a human heart and psyche.

Hardly aware of what I was at, I was on the phone to almost everyone whose number I had: the merest acquaintance, the gardaí, two veterinary surgeons, gossip columnists and for the second or third time to the Home for Strays (dogs and cats).

Fear took over. If previously I had believed I had learnt all about fear that was known, I saw how mistaken I had been. I now feared fully and extensively. I feared for those who cannot defend themselves, for the born failures, the innocent, the habitual victims, those who for various reasons are never caught in the net of compassion.

Then—at the third or fourth phone call to the Home for Strays— there came a woman's voice, another one, yes, a cat of the breed and colour I had described had been brought in.

And yet ... I mustn't give way, by which I mean I dare not believe that the miracle had happened and Sabrina was raised from the dead.

I took a taxi to the animal shelter, not trusting myself to drive the car soberly.

What might I see? A blurred image of a beige and brown-tipped little creature who ignored my high-toned greeting? No. Before I could open my mouth I heard two extended miaos.

I stooped and with one hand under the warm familiar belly picked up Sabrina and sat down with her perched by her claws on my lap. All was well, all manner of things shall be well, quoted—did she?—the freckled woman in the distance, not a very far distance.

I had been granted a vision comparable to what I believed was that of the Ark of the Covenant.

If this was a serial, I could end this instalment with "And then a most extraordinary thing happened." But, as it is closer to the diary form, I shall rely on the notes I made at the time. The woman—I am not certain how we came to speak of something other than what had brought me there—told me, casually, as if it was the coincidence that was notable, that she was in much the same situation as Sabrina, that in fact she was a human waif and stray (she didn't quite put it like that), not waiting either to be claimed or done away with—it wouldn't come to such an extreme—but with no clear future in sight.

This is a diary as I never tire—if the reader does—of reiterating. So what did I experience in those few days? Hopelessness, loss of all trust in a divine or semi-benign providence. But I could indulge in such reflections or speculations.

What of the millions, billions, of men and women who along the ages were in the throes of such acute bodily agony, from the medieval plagues to Altzheimer's disease, other manifestations of pre-senile decay and cancer? In such overwhelming physical distress there is no possibility of any approach to thinking.

Are we then the victims of a cruel, sadistic sustainer of the cosmos? A question asked by the recorders and prophets of old. I am thinking of the Old Testament, the Pentateuch.

Some pointed out that this God, Jahwez, subjected his Son, the Second Person of the Trinity, to unspeakable agonies. No, not so, they were not unspeakable in the manner I describe, they did not banish consciousness, rather, as mental or psychic pain does, extended it.

How far does the Gospel Jesus go in recognising, if not explaining or justifying, this?

"I am come not to bring peace but a sword"; "Many are called but few are chosen"; "There shall be weeping and gnashing of teeth"?

As I jot down these notes I see a not very wide, slow-flowing river between deep banks. I try to follow it past where I am but cannot. I mention this for what significance, if any, it may have. If an attempt at reassurance, despite the foregoing, a very feeble and ineffective one.

If we find ourselves on this earth where we never chose to be—were not consulted—what justification can there be for subjecting us to frightful torment? None, as far as I can see.

As I indicated little or none of this might have struck me, had it not been for the disappearance of the cat.

Beige ... There are times when colour is everything. At the Home for Strays would it blaze out?—a manner of speaking for it is a subdued shade with darker tips—among the blacks, whites, black and whites, brindles? They had been unclear on the phone, though had the most precise information about whatever been communicated to me, I would have found it confusing or downright unintelligible.

Yes ... as Mr and Mrs Fussenegger have impatiently guessed—no relation to their great compatriot, she was there!

If miracles take place, and they do, it is not in isolation but in small clusters or as if simultaneously although this is illusion because simultaneity never comes to pass in the order of reality. The woman from whose arms I took Sabrina followed her, not into my embrace, no, let's say into my heart and psyche. Not young, she introduced herself as Amelia Lappski and thereafter became Melly.

There we are: a long way from King David dancing before the Ark of the Covenant perhaps, and again perhaps not.

I have a human as well as an animal companion, a blissful condition. However I am not blissful or I would here and now terminate this diary (which I'll do soon in any case) because, as Tolstoy wrote: "Happy families have no history." I'm as disturbed as before. That I am one of those spared the physical torment of the damned disturbs me. It puts me, with Melly, among the arbiters, those who may take a balanced view of reality, personal and cosmic.

Instead, I shall briefly relate our life in this leafy suburb, yes, I insist on the leaves though at the present — December — they are nearly all on the ground. Coming up to Christmas, but Melly's two adult children, one a woman, won't be visiting us.

Here I shall end this diary as I began: confused, emotionally and physically disturbed, filled by vast glimpses, by near visions, but finding each year and month, almost day, ever more difficult.

As a postscript let me add: Yes, it was her, out of all likelihood, as I have learned to understand the word, the pale beige and dark-chocolate tipped creature I caught an ecstatic glimpse of, before they showed it to me, was Sabrina.

This was a moment I cannot describe, more important than finding the Ark. She was the Ark.